CHRISTMAS Co

ay

LIS7b

by John Wardle

Published by
Christopher Vine 2011

Printed by The Amadeus Press
Copyright © 2011 Christopher Vine

ISBN 978-0-9553359-5-2

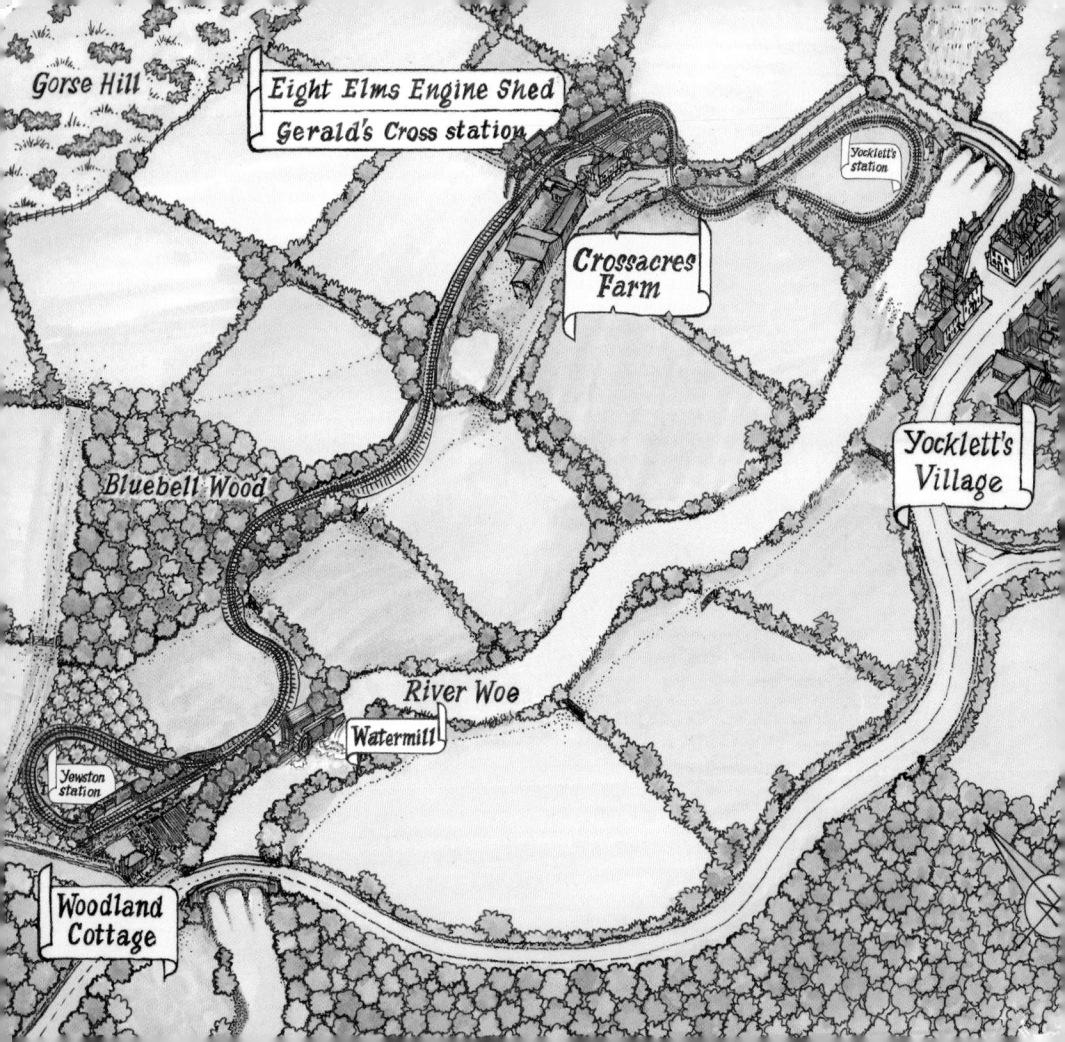

The Peter's Railway Series

Peter and his Grandpa have built an amazing miniature steam railway between their houses; Woodland Cottage and Crossacres Farm. The line even runs to Yockletts Village where Peter goes to school.

The locomotive, Fiery Fox, is a wonderful machine. Bright green and very powerful.

There have been many adventures on the railway and Peter and Grandpa have spent countless happy hours building it, together with their other projects.

The watermill electric generator is especially handy in this Christmas tale!

Christmas Steam

Each December, for at least a hundred years, the people of Yockletts have built a splendid grotto for Santa in the village hall. It has become a part of Christmas, just like singing carols and eating too much!

Unfortunately, the local council have decided to close the hall to save money. It didn't cost much to run, but they closed it anyway.

With no hall, there would be no grotto, and with no grotto there would be no Santa.

Kitty and Harry, Peter's little twin sister and brother, were very upset and so were all their friends. They simply could not understand it.

It was going to be a miserable Christmas.

But Peter had an idea. He and Grandpa could build a grotto in Bluebell Wood and take the children to visit Santa on their steam railway.

"That's brilliant," agreed Grandpa instantly. "We will run the trains on Christmas Eve."

The two heroes then spent ages plotting how they could make the journey a magical adventure.

"We will have to tell everyone it's going to happen," said Peter. "I'll draw some large posters and put them up at school and around the village."

When people saw the posters, they all wondered what was going on. Whatever were Peter and Grandpa up to?

"You will have to wait and see," was all Peter would say.....

Attention
Children
CHRISTMAS
IS NOT
CANCELLED!
come along to
YOCKLETTS
STATION
at 4pm on
CHRISTMAS
EVE

A few days before Christmas, Peter and Grandpa got to work building the grotto. Grandpa's idea was to use bales of straw to make the walls, like huge bricks. They could put a large waterproof sheet, or tarpaulin, over the top to keep any rain out.

Of course they used the railway to transport everything. Peter lit the fire in Fiery Fox and, while he looked after the engine, Grandpa carried the materials from the barn to the railway.

After carrying some forty bales of straw, he was quite tired and pleased to be able to sit on the train while Peter drove. Up and down the line they went, delivering them to the building site in Bluebell Wood.

It didn't take long to construct the little building, and pulling the tarpaulin over the top made it quite cosy inside. Grandpa found a branch from an old tree, which he set inside the grotto to hold the roof up like a tent. Now, if it rained, the water would run off the sides rather than dripping on Santa's head.

They made everything secure, by tying the tarpaulin to some trees with long bits of string. Now it wouldn't blow away if it was windy.

With the building finished, it was time to put up some decorations. Peter's Mum and Dad had agreed to help with this, so the two builders drove the train down to the station at Woodland Cottage, to pick them up.

Jo and Colin, Peter's mum and dad, were already waiting for them on the station platform. They had boxes and boxes of things to put up to make Santa feel welcome. One box had a long string of coloured lights which would look lovely in the night, but there was one small problem: There wasn't any electricity in Bluebell Wood.

"Why don't we run a cable up from the generator in the watermill?" asked Peter, when they were back at the farm. "It would be a shame not to have the lights working."

"Of course you're right," agreed Grandpa. "I don't think I have ever seen a Santa's grotto which isn't brightly lit. I'll have to find a very long piece of electric cable."

Grandpa found a reel of wire in his workshop; it had been left over from one of their previous projects. So while Jo and Colin were putting up decorations, he and Peter set up the cable between the mill and the grotto.

Grandpa didn't want to have any mains voltage wires or plugs outside, where they could get wet in the rain. So he decided to put the transformer-adapter in the watermill building, where it would be dry. Then it was a simple matter of connecting the adapter to one end of the long cable and the lights to the other end.

All the outside wiring would be low voltage and not dangerous at all. It wouldn't do to give Santa an electric shock!

Christmas Eve was a beautiful day and there had even been a light dusting of snow during the night. Not enough to make it difficult to run the trains, but it made the countryside look just like a Christmas card. The first train would leave Yockletts station at four o'clock, when it was just starting to get dark.

Peter and Grandpa pushed Fiery Fox out of Eight Elms engine shed, checked the water level in the boiler and lit the fire. While it was getting hot, they filled the tender with coal and water, ready for the evening's running.

The flames in the fire were getting brighter and hotter. Soon the boiler began to sizzle and sing like a kettle. Fiery Fox was waking up.

At a quarter to four, Peter steamed slowly out of the station. Grandpa was on the guard's van at the back. Passing through Grandma's garden they swept round some curves, and over the drive on the level crossing. A few minutes steaming through fields brought them in to Yockletts station.

What a crowd was waiting for them. All the young children from the village were there, and Kitty and Harry of course.

While the first ten children got onto the train, Peter made some adjustments to the controls in the cab and checked that the fire was burning brightly. He didn't want it to go out half way along the line.

Clouds of steam drifted in the evening air.

When everyone was sitting safely, Grandpa blew his guard's whistle. Peter gave a terrific answering blast on Fiery Fox's steam whistle and carefully opened her regulator. The train slid out of the station and ran along beside the river for a while, then gathered speed and climbed the gradient across the field.

Her exhaust roared as Fiery Fox hauled on the train. Faster and faster. Higher and higher.

Soon they were running at a cracking pace, back past the garden, through the farm yard, round the duck pond and then into Bluebell Wood. It was quite dark in there and Peter had to slow down a little, as the track wound its curvy route around the old trees.

They passed Santa's grotto but nobody on the train even noticed it. Peter and Grandpa had cunningly positioned the grotto so that it could not be seen on the outward journey.

A few moments later and the train rushed out of the wood, surging along the line. On and on they went, round the loop in Peter's garden and then back again towards the wood.

This time as they wound their way through the trees, the grotto seemed to appear out of the dark, as if by magic. Gloriously lit up by hundreds of tiny lamps, it looked wonderful. And right beside was a little fenced off pen with some reindeer, quietly standing by. (Grandpa had borrowed them from the local zoo!)

Peter put the brakes on and brought the train to a stop just at the front. The children were so amazed they could hardly speak.

Santa was standing at the entrance. "Welcome to my woodland grotto," he announced in a loud, but friendly voice. "Do come inside."

He turned and went in, but then came back out again. "I am ever so sorry," he apologised, "but I forgot something....."

"I forgot to say Ho Ho Ho!" he chortled, and went back inside.

They all got off the train and, one by one, went in to see Santa. The children who were waiting outside talked to the reindeer and patted their noses over the fence.

Peter and Grandpa ran trips on the train until every last child had been on the night-time steam adventure.

When the train took them home and pulled into Yockletts station, there was one last surprise: Grandma was on the platform, roasting chestnuts, marshmallows and sausages on an open fire. Delicious!

The children would remember this Christmas Eve for the rest of their lives.

Happy Christmas from Peter's Railway!

The End.

Why Peter's Railway?

Since a very small boy, Chris has always loved anything mechanical and especially steam engines. The first workshop was in his bedroom where he made an electric go-kart aged 8, followed by a mini-bike powered by the engine from a petrol lawn mower.

He spent many holidays on a friend's farm where there was a miniature railway across a field and so started a love of making model steam locomotives. The latest is Bongo, 8 feet long and the inspiration for Fiery Fox in the books.

Chris wanted to share his love and knowledge of railways and engineering: Peter's Railway is the result.

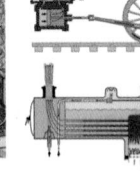
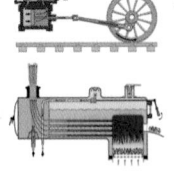

Story   **Technical**   **Adventure**

The original books

The original four books tell the charming story of Peter and his Grandpa building and running their steam railway across the farm. At the ends of chapters are special how-it-works pages with simple (but accurate) explanations of what has been happening in the story. In addition, Grandpa tells some fantastic stories from the old days on the railways. Age range 6 - 12 years approx.

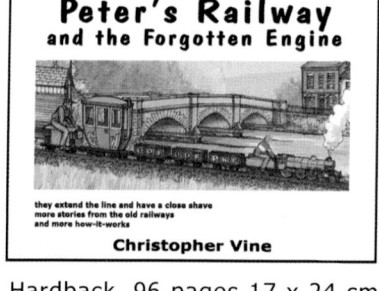

Hardback, 96 pages 17 x 24 cm with 30 watercolour pictures by John Wardle and 14 pages of clearly explained technical drawings. £11.99

New! Small format books

A new series of Peter's Railway in a smaller format. While the original books each contain several story or adventure threads, separate technical pages and Grandpa's tales, the small books concentrate on one aspect; a Peter's adventure, a Grandpa's tale of the old railways or a technical book.

'Little Peter's Railway' are gentle stories for younger children.

Little
**Peter's Railway
Christmas Steam**
Peter saves Christmas

Little
**Peter's Railway
Surprise Goods**
A bed-time story with a twist....

**Peter's Railway
A Bit of Energy**
Grandpa tries to answer a tricky question

**Peter's Railway
A Dark and Stormy Night**
Grandpa tells a tale from the old days

Paperbacks with 32 pages, 12 watercolour pictures - £2.99